VeggieTales

A Hoppy Easter

WORTHY® kids

ISBN 978-1-61795-485-6

Published by Worthy Kids, an imprint of Worthy Publishing Group, a division of Worthy Media, Inc.
Brentwood, Tennessee 37027
www.worthypublishing.com

Written and Designed by Bart Dawson
Illustrated by Lisa Reed and Lisa Wallace

Printed and bound in the United States of America

LBP_Jan15_1

On Easter Day, as Bob headed to the park for a picnic with friends, he heard a familiar voice behind him shout,

"Hoppy Easter!"

"Don't you mean 'Happy Easter'?"
asked Bob, turning to greet Larry.
"I like '**hoppy**' better," said Larry.
"It's more fun to say!"

Larry wiggled his bunny ears. "Are you ready for the

Super-Duper
Hoppy Easter Egg Hunt, Bob?

Mr. Lunt hid eggs for us to find on our way to the picnic."

"Wow, Larry, that sounds like fun!
But you know there's more to Easter than
chocolate and bunnies and eggs, right?
Easter is a celebration of God's love for each of us,"
explained Bob.

"Of course I know that, Bob," said Larry. "Now let's go find some eggs!"

Bob said, "Maybe for each egg we find, we can think of a way God shows his love."

"That's a **super-duper idea**, Bob," Larry said, as he unwrapped a chocolate bunny.

"Look, there's an egg right there! And I know the first way God shows his love for us." said Bob. "He made each of us unique. And we are all wonderfully made by him!"

"For sure," said Larry. "Let's go find some more eggs!"

As they continued toward the park,
Bob and Larry met Laura Carrot.

"Happy Easter!" said Laura. "What are
you doing?"

"**Hoppy Easter**, Laura," said Larry.

"We're hunting for Easter eggs," said Bob, "and sharing ways that God shows his love for us."

"That sounds like fun," said Laura, giggling at Larry's bunny ears.

"Found one!" cried Larry, holding up an egg.

"I know a way God shows his love for us," Laura said. "He watches over us and keeps us safe."

"That's very true," said Petunia, joining the group.

"**Hoppy Easter**, Petunia!" shouted Larry. "Do you want to join us?"

"**Hoppy Easter** to all of you," said Petunia. "I'd love to."

After a few minutes of searching,
Laura exclaimed, "I found one!"
"Way to go, Laura," said Bob.

"Oh, I know another way God shows his love for us," Petunia said. "He provides us with everything we need."

"Mmmmm, like chocolate bunnies," Larry said, nibbling the bunny's ear.

"Well, yes, but he gives us many more blessings in our life than just chocolate," replied Bob.

Soon Junior came over to see what they were looking for.

"Hoppy Easter!" cried Larry.

"Do you need help finding something?" asked Junior.
"We are hunting for Easter eggs," Bob said.

"I see one!" Junior cried.
"Good job," said Bob.

"And for each egg we find, we're also sharing a way God shows his love for us. Do you know one?" Bob asked.

"Well, God gave us the Bible so we could learn and get to know all about him," said Junior.

"I see another egg by the tree!" said Laura excitedly.
"Egg-cellent," Larry said, and they all laughed.

Laura said, "And God shows his love by always being with us."

"Yes, that's true!" agreed Junior.

"Oh look, there's an egg up on that branch," said Junior, hopping up and down.

"I know another way God shows his love for us," Petunia said. "Just look around you. He gave us this beautiful world to live in."

"You are so right!" Laura added. "Just look at the blue sky, the beautiful flowers, and green grass all around us."

Soon, Madame Blueberry came over
to see what the others were doing.
When Bob explained, she said,
"That sounds like fun."

"**It's super-duper, hoppy fun!**" exclaimed Larry.

"I found one, right over here!" Petunia said.

"Great!" said Madame Blueberry. "And I know a way God shows his love for us. When we do wrong things, we can say we're sorry to God, and he forgives us!"

"Hey!" laughed Junior, as Rooney, the dog, ran up to him with an egg in his mouth.

"Rooney found an egg!" cried Jimmy and Jerry as they caught up to the dog.

"**Hoppy Easter!**" said Larry. "Do you guys know a way God shows his love for us?"

"Sure," Jimmy answered. "God likes it when we pray, and he hears our prayers."

"Yeah, he hears our prayers!" agreed Jerry.

"Did you find ten eggs?" asked Mr. Lunt as he joined the group.

"Not yet," replied Larry. "We've only found eight so far."

"Make that nine," said Bob. "I see one in the hole in that tree!"

"And I know another way God shows his love for us," Larry said. "He gives us friends and family who care for us, and," he added with a big grin, "to have a

Hoppy Easter Picnic with!"

Bob said, "But the greatest way God showed his love for us was by sending Jesus, his Son, who gave his life to save us."

They all nodded in agreement. Larry said, "And that's why we celebrate Easter."

Then Junior said, "Now, let's find that last egg." His stomach growled. "I'm getting hungry."

As they searched for the last egg,
Mr. Lunt chuckled to himself.
"What's so funny, Mr. Lunt?"
asked Petunia.

He, he, he, he, he . . .

"Oh, nothing . . . I just know where
the last egg is," he said, lifting his hat.
"Oh, Mr. Lunt!" giggled Laura.

God showed how much he loved us
by sending his one and only Son
into the world so that we might have
eternal life through him.
1 John 4:9 (NLT)